Millersburg Magick Mysteries #4

Feline Navidad

Suzan Harden

FELINE NAVIDAD (Millersburg Magick Mysteries #4)
Copyright © 2025 by Angry Sheep Publishing, LLC
All rights reserved.

ISBN-13 – 978-1-64918-066-7

Published by Angry Sheep Publishing, LLC
Findlay, Ohio

Interior Design by JW Manus
Cover Design by Elaina Lee

*To Thunderbird and D.C., the best cats
a family could ask for*

More books by Suzan Harden
(Each series is in suggested reading order)

BLOODLINES

Blood Magick
Zombie Love
Zombie Confidential
Zombie Wedding
Amish, Vamps & Thieves
Blood Sacrifice
Love, War & a Bulldog
Zombie Goddess
Ravaged
Sacrificed
Reality Bites
Ghouls in the Grocery
Resurrected
Bloodlines Shorts Anthology
Bloodlines: The First Boxed Set

SEASONS OF MAGICK

Spring
Summer
Autumn
Winter
The Seasons of Magick Anthology

CROSSOVER WORLDS

Invasion!

JUSTICE

Sword and Sorceress 28
("Justice")
Sword and Sorceress 30
("Diplomacy in the Dark")
Justice: The Beginning
A Question of Balance
A Modicum of Truth
A Matter of Death
A Touch of Mother
A Twist of Love
A Virtue of Child
A Hand of Father
A Measure of Knowledge
A Hint of Thief
A Cup of Conflict
A Barrel of Vintner
A Sprout of Wild
A Glimmer of Light

THE JUSTICE THALIA STORIES

Snowfall
Murder Most Fowl
The Sweetest Poison
A Granddaughter of Mine
Too Many Fish in the Sea

TALES OF THE TWELVE

The Trickster Priestess and the Demon

888-555-HERO

Hero De Facto
Hero Ad Hoc
Hero De Novo
A Very Hero Christmas
Hero De Jure
Hero In Camera
Hero Amicus Curiae
A Very Hero Wedding
A Very Hero New Year
Hero Ad Litem
Queer Eye for the Super Guy

SOLAR SYSTEM SERVICES, INC.

Alone Is Not Lonely
Halloween Harvest
("A Place at the Table")
A Place at the Table

MILLERSBURG MAGICK MYSTERIES

Spells and Sleuths
Fae and Felonies
Magick and Murder
Feline Navidad

SOCCER MOMS OF THE APOCALYPSE

Pestilence in Pumpkin Spice
Famine in French Vanilla
War in White Chocolate
Death in Double Mocha
Demons Run at Halloween

MISCELLANEOUS

Sword and Sorceress 31
("Pig-Headed")
Sword and Sorceress 32
("Unexpected")
Practical Witches
Revenge Served Hot
The Yule Switch
Chocolate for Dinner
Silver Shoes and Pigs' Ears
Snipe Hunt

For updates, news, and giveaways, join Suzan's mailing list (suzanharden. blogspot.com/p/contact-me.html) or visit her website at suzanharden.com. You can also check her out @SuzanHardenWriter on Facebook.

Chapter 1

Anxiety jittered along Teller's nerves as he stalked into Penn's room. His brother sprawled across the pink duvet on the bed he shared with his human Kaley. In other words, Penn's usual spot when he wasn't demanding their humans serve him extra portions of food. Teller leapt onto the mattress and rubbed his cheek against Penn's golden face, hoping to wake him gently.

Only to receive a swat.

At least, Penn hadn't used his claws.

"The girls aren't home yet," Teller said.

"You woke me up to tell me an obvious fact?" Penn yawned and stretched.

"Their winter break starts today. They should be home from school by now." Teller understood this

7

school was where their humans learned human things, but he never understood why their dam Rachel didn't teach her kits such skills. The idea of a mother cat relying on other felines to teach her kits was rather bizarre.

Not that his and Penn's own dam really had a chance to teach them before they were taken away. He barely remembered her anyway, other than she was gold with darker gold stripes like Penn.

Teller jumped onto Kaley's nightstand and stared out the window overlooking the street. The leaves had long since fallen from the ancient maple tree in the front yard. Gray clouds masked the sun. Under the soft glow of holiday lights, the asphalt pavement gleamed from the mix of rain and sleet. No human vehicles had rolled up or down the street for quite a while.

A faint chill penetrated the glass and made his breath fog on the pane. Only dogs were stupid enough to go outside on days like this. Even cats without a human were smart enough to find a cozy spot and sleep the dreary afternoon away.

"Technically, winter break starts tomorrow." Penn joined Teller on the nightstand. "They're fine. I would know otherwise."

"You're not properly bonded with your witch any more than I am with mine," Teller growled.

8

Penn snorted and ignored the obvious. "Lie to your-self, but don't lie to me. You're impatient for them to set up the new tree course."

"Well, it was courteous for Ellie and River to deliver an evergreen after the two-shape failed to help our humans bring one home this year."

"Are you still moping about Donny? You've always tolerated him before."

"That was before the two-form started sniffing around my human." Teller refused to use the two-form's personal name.

"Maybe Kirsten likes slumming it with a canine."

For that remark, Teller knocked his brother off the wooden surface. Penn shrieked and landed with a thump on the rug.

"You jerk!" But rather than attacking, Penn licked the golden fur of his sides and paws back into place. Momma always said to be neat, one of the few things Teller remembered her saying, but his brother took fastidiousness to a new level.

"At least, my human picked a two-shape," Teller spat. "Yours doesn't have the sense to stay away from the halfling."

"The sidhe are the reason the two-shapes exist," Penn shot back.

Teller returned to watching for their humans. "All I'm saying is Kirsten could have picked a feline two-shape."

"And where was she going to find one?" Penn didn't bother rejoining Teller on the nightstand. "There are no prides nearby for her to choose from."

Teller's ears flicked. The familiar hum of their humans' specific metal and plastic vehicle had turned onto the asphalt path that ran in front of their house. He leapt down from the nightstand and padded out of his brother's room.

He reached the rug at the bottom of the staircase when Penn yowled, "Banzai!"

Teller was already rolling, anticipating his brother's pounce. They swatted each other until the hinges on the back door squeaked.

Teller smoothly rose to his paws. "Are we done?"

Penn glared at him. "Don't knock me off a perch again."

Teller sniffed before he turned and stalked through the living room and into the kitchen. Penn trotted behind him. The delicious scent of breakfast bacon still lingered in the air from this morning.

"There you two are," Kaley said cheerfully as she hung her thick outwear on one of the pegs sticking out of the wall for that purpose. "That must have been one serious nap you were taking."

"Penn was," Teller said. "Not me." He passed his brother's human and approached his own. "You're late."

"Hey, sweet'ums." Kirsten lifted him into her arms and kissed the top of his head. Unfortunately, she reeked of the two-form who courted her.

Teller sneezed.

"You're not getting sick, are you?" She cradled him and scratched his favorite place on his neck.

"Just allergies to your possible mate." However, he was getting the attention he'd been craving since the last full moon. A purr rumbled through his chest.

"Hey, Kirsten?" her sister called. Penn sat next to his human at the entrance to the living room, snickering. "Come see this!"

Teller's human stopped scratching his neck and joined her sibling. "What the—?"

The annual dead evergreen stood in its red bowl of water before the huge front window facing the street. No ornaments or lights hung from it yet. But once the humans decorated it, the annual climbing competition between him and Penn would commence.

Ellie had found the picture album. She and River

moved the couch, chairs, and coffee table to places that the twins' dam had dictated over the years.

"Where did that come from? I thought Mom and Dad decided against having a tree this year," Kirsten muttered. "Not that they asked us."

"Well, I sure wasn't going back out to the Slaughter's tree farm," Kaley said as she stared at the white pine. "Goddess. I'm still having nightmares about tripping over Warren Simon's body."

"Wonder what changed their mind?" Kirsten asked.

"They didn't," Teller said.

Kirsten ignored him per usual and set him on the living room rug before she pulled her phone out of her front jeans pocket. She frowned when her mother's artificial voice started talking.

"Hey, mom! Glad you and Dad changed your minds about getting a tree for the holidays. We'll have both dinner and the box of decorations ready by the time you and Dad get home." She touched the glass on her phone and shoved it back in her pocket.

"Ellie and River really should have told our humans about their plan before they set up this annual sacrifice," Teller said. "I can't believe you told the halfling where our humans kept the water bowl for dead trees."

"He asked politely." Penn twitched his tail. "And he smells so nice."

12

Teller growled low in his throat. "Should Kaley allow him to court her, you will not be part of it."

Penn sniffed. "Doctor Ethan thinks so."

"He doesn't know you are fawning over River because he smells like catnip to you," Teller shot back. "And the fool is accidentally emitting the odor in order to make you like him."

"Or maybe he's doing it on purpose to please me," Penn mocked.

"He's not that bright."

"You're confusing Donny's lack of intelligence with River's natural brilliance."

"Brilliance, my fluffy tail," Teller muttered.

Kirsten's phone rang. "Hey, Mom."

Rachel Wilson shrieked a number of rude invectives before she said, "I did not bring any pine tree home."

"But Yule is tomorrow," Kirsten said.

"Get out of the house! Now!" Rachel demanded.

"Did she really just say that?" Kaley rolled her eyes.

"It's a gift," Teller said. As usual, the twins ignored him. His human could barely communicate with him in the best of times. Now, her dam was getting her riled to the point he couldn't get through to her.

"Mom, if you didn't put up the tree, maybe Dad did," Kirsten said.

"Get the cats, get in the car, and come over to my office," Rachel demanded.

"Fine, Mom, but we're stopping at Jo's to get coffee and a snack first," Kirsten replied. "See you in a bit."

Kaley knelt next to the tree and extended her palms. Penn hoped up on her shoulder to observe.

Energy whispered along Teller's fur, even the fine hairs around his nose, and he sneezed again.

Kirsten picked him up again. "Maybe we should take you in to see Dad. I know you got your flu vaccine, but I don't want you sick for tomorrow."

"Yeah, he's sick in the head," Penn muttered.

"I agree, Snookums." Kaley carefully got to her feet so she wouldn't dislodge Penn. "We don't detect any magick in or around the tree."

"Let's swing by Dad's clinic first," Kirsten said. "We can have him check out Teller's sneezing and ask him about the tree."

"But we're taking both cats, right?" Kaley asked.

"That's what Mom said to do," Kirsten replied with a thick layer of resentment.

Teller wanted to protest, but he knew it wouldn't do any good. The last time he tried, his human's dam had paralyzed him with a spell and shoved him into his carrier anyway. Last thing he wanted was Kirsten to learn that trick.

"Kirsten, I don't think there's anything wrong with your cat." Doctor Ethan held the flat disk of his stethoscope against Teller's chest. At least, he had the courtesy of warming it between his hands first.

"That's what I tried to tell her," Teller said.

"At least, you're out of your carrier," Penn's muffle voice shot back.

Teller tolerated his human's sire running his hands all over Teller's body. One of the best things about Doctor Ethan was his gentleness. His partners at the clinic could be rough during an exam. All of the non-humans in Millersburg preferred Doctor Ethan because if his acknowledgement of their feelings, even if he couldn't speak their languages.

"Has Teller vomited at home?" he asked.

"No—" Kirsten started.

"But we didn't check the whole house," Kaley interjected. "We were too busy checking out the tree."

Doctor Ethan frowned. "What tree? Did the maple lose a limb?"

"No," Kirsten said. "The white pine you set up in the living room for Yule."

He released Teller. "I didn't set up any tree."

Teller strode across the examination table, looked up at his human, projected an image of Ellie and River. She ignored him yet again.

"Well, if Mom didn't and you didn't and we didn't, who did?" Kaley asked.

"Your Aunt Jo and Uncle Jimmy both have keys to the house." Doctor Ethan shrugged. "Have you checked with either of them?"

"Not yet," Kaley said. "We need to check with Donny. He has one, too."

"Maybe I should to get that one back," Doctor Ethan teased.

"Yes, you should," Teller said with fervor. Again, Kirsten ignored him as did Doctor Ethan. This was getting a little ridiculous. Kirsten was nearly an adult by human measures, but despite his efforts, they still hadn't formed a proper witch-familiar link.

"He hasn't abused the privilege before now," she said pointedly to her sire. "Do you really think he'd tick you off by sneaking into our house after all your threats of castrating him while he was in his coyote form?"

"I wasn't serious until you two started dating." Doctor Ethan smirked.

Teller walked back to Doctor Ethan, purred, and

rubbed his head against Doctor Ethan's arm. Unfortunately, his human's sire didn't understand the feline encouragement to keep the canine two-form out of the Wilson house or prevent him from mating with Kirsten. Instead, Doctor Ethan scratched behind Teller's ears.

Penn rolled in his carrier, laughing his butt off.

"Stop it," Teller growled.

"Sorry, little dude. I didn't mean to upset you." Doctor Ethan stopped scratching behind Teller's ears, which made Penn laugh even harder. "It's probably just dust in the house, Kirsten. He's not showing signs of being sick."

Teller debated whether now would be a good time to upchuck a hair ball. Unfortunately, Doctor Ethan may decide to keep him at the clinic if his midafternoon snack came up as well.

"Did you detect any spells on the tree?" Doctor Ethan asked.

"None whatsoever," Kaley stated.

"It sounds like something Jimmy would do." Doctor Ethan rubbed his chin. "Give him a call. Tell him if he's breaking and entering my home, he owes me a six-pack."

"Are you sure nothing's wrong with Teller?" Kirsten asked.

"Sweetie, he's fine. I'm sure it's just dust."

Or a stupid canine two-form, but Teller kept that to himself.

"But you're more in tune with him than I am." Doctor Ethan ran his hand along Teller's back. "Does he feel distressed to you?"

Kirsten narrowed her eyes.

Teller wasn't ready for her abrupt mental contact. Before he could concentrate on Ellie, River, and the tree, Kirsten jumped back.

"Wow. I was not expecting that." She blinked to clear her head.

Dog feces! Teller hid his face against Doctor Ethan's abdomen. He really screwed up.

"What's wrong?" Doctor Ethan asked.

"Teller hates Donny as much as you do," Kirsten blurted.

"That's not true," both Teller and Doctor Ethan said at the same time.

"Really?" Kirsten crossed her arms and stared at her sire.

"In Teller's case, he might be a little jealous," Doctor Ethan said. "You've been paying more attention to your boyfriend than to him."

"Oh, sure, blame it all on me," Teller muttered.

"So, I'm not paying enough attention to you either?" Kirsten grumbled.

"It's not that." Doctor Ethan bared his teeth.

Teller backed away from him and crouched in front of Kirsten, ready to pounce if her sire tried to attack her.

"You both will always be our babies," Doctor Ethan said. "It's just a little hard to let go now that you've grown up."

Kirsten willingly flung herself into her sire's arms. "You know we'll always love you, Dad."

Teller flicked his tail. Humans were so weird. They bared their teeth when they were happy. And grappled with each other to show affection. He would never understand them. The two-form made more sense.

"If you two are finished hugging it out, can we go please go to Jo's?" Kaley whined. "I'm starving."

"Starving?" Doctor Ethan released Kirsten.

"It's what happens when we eat breakfast at six-thirty in the morning and lunch at ten-thirty," Kaley complained.

"Back into the carrier, Teller." Kirsten lifted the plastic box onto the table.

As much as Teller hated being hauled around in the dang carrier, he acceded to her wish because it was the fastest way to get home and get out of the plastic box.

Even if they went to see the sister of Kirsten's dam's dam first, she always kept treats for Teller and his brother.

The girls exited the clinic and settled the carriers on the back seat of their vehicle.

"Give me the keys," Kaley demanded.

"Why?"

Teller couldn't see his human's face, but her voice indicated her irritation.

"I'll drive while you call Uncle Jimmy and Donny."

"Fine." The keys jingled before his human climbed into the front passenger seat. She pulled out her phone while her sister started the vehicle.

"You really screwed up," Penn hissed. "Breaking the trust of your witch—"

"Shut up," Teller yowled back.

Kirsten peered around the edge of her seat. "You okay, big guy?"

"I'm fine," he said. That seemed to reassure her. He curled into a ball in the back of the carrier. At least, he had some time on the ride. He needed to figure out how to fix things with his human.

Chapter 2

Teller still hadn't conceived of a plan to remedy things with his witch before they arrived at the coffee shop. However, Kirsten managed one call on the ride. Uncle Jimmy denied leaving anything at the Wilson house. He pointed out he would have most certainly left a note demanding a six-pack from Doctor Ethan if he had brought a Yule tree to their house, moved all the furniture, and set it up in the living room. The two-form didn't answer her call.

When Kirsten carried Teller into the food and drink shop, he immediately got a whiff of the two-form. Speak of the devil.

The musky odor overwhelmed the incredible scent of bacon, and Teller sneezed again. Of course, Kirsten strode straight over to the table where the two-form sat and kissed him. Teller gagged.

"What a drama king," Penn grumbled.

"It was a reflex," Teller shot back. "I think I have a hairball." That was the story he was sticking with no matter what teasing his brother dished out.

"What are you doing here?" Kirsten said. "I've been trying to call you."

Great Cat above! She used the same tone with the two-form she used to reserve for only him. Maybe Penn was right. Maybe he was jealous of the two-form. Not that he'd ever admit such a thing to his brother.

"I needed internet access to research a paper, and they kicked me out of the school library." The two-form laughed. "Even the teachers and staff wanted the heck out of the building for winter break. I wasn't ignoring you. I had to turn off my phone to concentrate. Greg has been blowing it up, even though I said I could not work this weekend. Tyson's wife went into labor, and the bar's short-handed for tonight."

"Well, I'm glad you're here," Kirsten said.

Teller gagged at the additional kissing noises. Why do mating humans feel the need to touch their lips and tongues together? It's so gross!

The two-form leaned over to look at him. "What's a matter, big guy? You got a hair ball bugging you?"

"That's not his problem," Kaley said from above. "He doesn't like you." Ceramic clinked on wood before she knelt and gave each cat a treat.

"Kaley!" Kirsten protested.

The two-form straightened, which irritated Teller. He wanted to see the two-form's reaction when his human told him the truth.

"Since when?" The two-form sounded puzzled. "We've always gotten along before."

Kaley stood and sat on the other side of the two-form. "You weren't dating my sister before this month."

Kirsten didn't say a word. Teller wasn't sure how to handle her betrayal. How could she let her littermate dictate the situation, instead of defending him?

Except he had accidentally let slip his true feelings to her about the two-form. Which brought him back to his original problem. How did he make up with his witch?

"Teller is jealous of me?" The two-form leaned over in his chair to look at Teller again. "Dude, you know I can't replace you. You're Kirsten's familiar."

"You damn well better remember that," Teller said.

"Here." The two-form reached up for the top of the table. "Want some bacon?" He stuck a bite-sized bit of heaven between the wires at the entrance of the carrier.

Teller was torn between his love of bacon and irritation that the two-form was trying to bribe him.

"I won't take her away from you, Teller." The two-form eyed him with an earnest expression. "I promise. Peace offering?"

"All right." Teller daintily took the tidbit. It was so delicious. He licked his muzzle. "It doesn't mean I like you for pursuing my human."

"I promise I won't do anything to hurt her," the two-form said.

"You'd better not," Teller said.

The two-form straightened in his chair.

"Do you understand him?" Kirsten asked.

"In a manner." The two-form laughed. "I'm going to need another job if I'm going to continue dating you."

"What?" Kirsten stammered. "I'm not asking you to—"

"Take it easy. I meant if I'm dating you, I'm also dating Teller in a way." The two-form slurped his drink. Typical canine. Couldn't eat or drink without making obnoxious noises. What did Kirsten see in someone with no manners?

"What are you talking about?" Kaley teased. "You guys become a threesome?"

Penn snickered in his own carrier.

"Shut up!" Teller yowled.

"No, it's more like when a guy wants to date my mom." The two-form slipped Teller another piece of bacon, which he reluctantly accepted. If only the two-form wasn't pursuing his human, he would feel much better about getting the tasty gift.

"They think sucking up to me will win me over," the two-form continued. "And I'll be on their side in convincing Mom to start a relationship with them."

"So, they stupidly think bribing a kid will get them laid?" Kirsten said incredulously.

"And you think our cats are that stupid?" From her tone, Kaley took it as offensively as Teller did.

"No familiar is that stupid." Teller recognized the boots of Jo, the sibling of Rachel's dam. More ceramic clinked on the wood above him. The sounds were followed by the sweet smell of honey and the sharper odor of herbs.

"And I never said Teller or Penn are stupid!" the two-form protested.

"Did you ask her?" Kirsten said.

"Too busy getting your coffee, thank you very much," Kaley retorted.

"Ask me what?" Jo said.

"Were you at our house earlier?" Kirsten asked.

"Not with Peggy out sick. Mary and I have been swamped since we opened this morning. Why do you think I've been to your place?"

"Someone set up a Yule tree in our living room," Kaley said.

"And it wasn't Mom or Dad or Uncle Jimmy," Kirsten added. "That was why I was trying to call you earlier."

"I didn't take a tree to your house," the two-form protested.

"What do you mean someone set up a Yule tree?" Jo asked.

"Someone put a six-foot white pine in our tree stand with water and set it in the front room window where Mom and Dad always put our live tree." Kaley said. "It was just waiting to be decorated. And all the furniture has been moved to the right places, so we figured it was someone we know."

"Were there any signs of a forced entry?" Jo asked.

"Not on the back door," Kirsten said. "We didn't check the front door."

"We didn't check any of the upstairs windows either," Kaley said.

"Let me guess." A sourness lay in Jo's voice. "Your mother freaked when you called her about the tree and told you to leave the house."

"How did you know?" Kirsten asked.

"She's been a little paranoid since she was framed for Warren Simon's murder right before Thanksgiving." Jo exhaled deeply.

Some time ago, Teller had noticed older humans do that when they were exasperated. Didn't they understand such a gesture only aggravated their offspring and made things worse?

"Really?" Sarcasm thickened Kaley's voice. "We hadn't noticed."

"And she called me and ordered me to let her know when you two got here," Jo added.

Teller cocked his head to listen intently to the humans conversation. Rachel commanding her elder? Was she making a play for dominance? But Jo had never threatened the kits or harmed them in any way.

Frankly, he wouldn't have blamed Rachel for killing anyone who threatened her kits. That was simply how the world worked sometimes.

He never expected life to be fair. If it were, he and Penn would have been adopted with their sisters instead of being sent to the prison for four-legs.

"I don't want to call her," Kaley said. "She's been impossible to talk to for the last three weeks."

"I already texted her," Jo said. "But you two need to

cut her some slack. If you kids and Jimmy hadn't figured out what was going on, she could have ended up in prison for life. Or worse. And she was terrified she would leave you girls and your father defenseless."

"Liked burned at the stake worse," the two-form said.

Kirsten gasped. "How could you say that?"

"It's not personal," the two-form said. "As far as Humanity Now is concerned, they'd be perfectly happy to shoot me through the heart with a silver bullet."

"Dad keeps telling her to chill, too," Kaley murmured. "But I'm afraid she's going to give herself a stroke with all her worrying."

"Well, she wouldn't worry so much if you two were more forthright about where you are," Jo said. "Speaking of which, where were you between leaving the house and coming here?"

"We took Teller to the clinic for Dad to check him out," Kirsten said. "He was sneezing a lot when we got home."

"He sneezed twice," Kaley corrected.

"At the house," Kirsten said. "He sneezed a third time when we entered the café."

The two-form slipped Teller a third chunk of bacon. He nibbled on his treat as he considered the situation. A familiar would have calmed Rachel over her fears, but his human and her sister hadn't been able to convince their mother to select another familiar since Morticia died a few years ago.

"I wanted to make sure Teller wasn't coming down with the flu," Kirsten said. "No one wants to be sick during Yule."

"I don't like the idea that someone was in your house," Jo murmured. "You girls stay here for now. I'll text both of your parents."

Her feet turned, and she walked toward the counter.

"Guess I got too excited about Mom and Dad changing their minds about getting a tree." Kaley sounded terribly sad, which was very much unlike her.

"It's all right. The tree is safe," Penn crooned. Unfortunately, his only acknowledgement was a bit of egg cooked with herbs on the tip of his human's finger.

"Neither of our witches are listening," Teller commented.

"Give me some of your bacon," Kaley demanded.

"Why?" the two-form said.

"Because you're giving some to Teller, and Penn is feeling left out," Kaley insisted.

"He just wants out of the carrier," Kirsten said.

"No, I don't!" Penn screeched. "I want some bleeping bacon!"

"'Bleeping'?" Teller mocked his brother.

"You know the dam doesn't allow swear words." Penn grumbled. "In any language. Remember what Old Morticia said."

Teller laughed. "You are such a kiss-ass."

"Here you go, Penn." The two-form leaned over and inserted a chunk of bacon between the wires of Penn's carrier.

"Ha!" His teeth crunched their favorite treat.

"I could have given it to him," Kaley complained.

"No, you wouldn't," Kirsten and the two-form at the same time.

"You would have eaten it," the two-form teased.

Kaley must have done something because Kirsten and the two-form burst out laughing.

"You two are just mean," Kaley complained.

"And you're just mad because you miss your lover boy," the two-form taunted.

"I do miss him," she said. "But it's important that he gets to know his relatives."

"I cannot even imagine that," Kirsten said.

"I can," the two-form muttered.

"What are you talking about?" Kirsten asked.

"Werecoyotes aren't exactly known for committing to one person," he answered.

"It's a choice," Kirsten said firmly. "Just because your dad made some bad choices in his life, it doesn't mean you will. You have a brain, and you have ambition. You're not taking illegal shortcuts."

"I may have done everything right, but I'm still getting screwed." His comment was followed by a thunk on the wood above Teller's carrier.

"Sometimes, it takes a while for the wheels of justice to turn," Kirsten said.

"Is there anymore bacon?" Penn whispered.

"I don't think so," Teller whispered back. "Now, shush." From what he understood from Kirsten, her parents, and the two-form, the money he had been granted for his further education had been taken away from him by the Normal authorities.

"I don't want to be starting college in my eighties," the two-form said.

"Wait a minute," Kaley said. "I thought you got an internship with the joint taskforce."

"I don't want—" The two-form was interrupted by Kirsten's phone ringing.

"Hey, Mom."

"Where are you girls?"

Even with the other patrons in the coffee shop, Teller could clearly hear Rachel. And she sounded furious.

"Teller was sneezing so we stopped at the clinic before we came to the café," Kirsten said, but Teller could feel the edge of her emotions. She was trying to bide by Jo's wishes and be considerate, but her dam's attitude ratcheted up her irritation. "Also, Jo told us to stay here while she texted you and Dad. We asked her about the tree at the house, but she wasn't the one who left it. Neither did Jimmy or Donny."

As Teller listened, he wished he could speak human for the first time in his life to reassure Kirsten she wasn't crazy. Nor could he blame her for her annoyance when her elders were jerking her north, south, east, and west.

"I just got Jo's text," Rachel said. "Stay with her until you hear from me."

"Yes, ma'am. We love you." Kirsten exhaled. "I am so glad I'm going to college soon."

"Your parents care about you," the two-form said roughly. "Don't throw that away because your mom's a little overprotective."

"Overprotective? Do you—" Kirsten abruptly stopped talking as footsteps approached their table. Teller caught a whiff of Jo's soap.

"Olivia is on her way here, and she and Mary are closing for me," the kinswoman said. "I'm meeting Jimmy over at your house."

"We're coming with you," Kaley proclaimed.

"Me, too," the two-form agreed. "If jerks are harassing the Wilsons again, you'll need someone who can track scents."

"I'm not giving you permission," Jo said. "But I can't stop you from going to your own home, and right now, we don't know for sure someone broke in until Jimmy checks the house."

"Mom ordered us to stay with you until we hear from her," Kirsten said with an air of innocence.

"That's stretching her request," Jo muttered.

"Still, your butt is sufficiently covered," Kirsten said. "I'll douse any fireball Mom throws at you."

"It was Ellie and River who left the tree," Teller howled.

The two-form leaned over to look at Teller. "Ellie and River did what?"

"What are you mumbling about Donny?" Jo asked.

The two-form straightened in his chair. "Teller's upset. Something about Ellie and River. My feline isn't as strong as my canine language skills."

"What's does either of them have to do with this?" Kirsten said. "They flew out this afternoon."

"When are they supposed to land?" Jo asked.

"Their plane is supposed to land in Vegas around

ten p.m. our time," Kaley said. "River said he'd text me when they arrive."

"Have you ever noticed he smells like catnip when he's at your house?" the two-form said.

"You go around sniffing other men?" Kirsten said.

"No, but I think if anyone's sucking up to your cats, it's him, not me. They would have attacked anyone who came into your house and was a threat to you girls and your parents."

Chair legs scooted across the linoleum floor, and human clothing rustled. The two-form picked up Teller's carrier.

"See you in the morning, Mary," Jo called out as she headed for the café's front doors.

"Good night," Mary said.

Teller liked Mary. She may not be a witch, but she had an affinity for her own cats. Real cats, who lived in the barn and hunted.

Not that he would give up sleeping in a warm bed with Kirsten. Though for once, he'd like to chase real prey and not practice on insects.

Now, if he could only figure out how to tell his witch the dang Yule tree wasn't a threat.

Chapter 3

Teller curled up and sulked in his carrier. Of course, Kirsten decided to ride back to the Wilson territory with the two-form in his machine. Which meant Teller was forced to accompanied them.

Noxious odors that had nothing to do with the two-form's natural musk came from underneath Teller's carrier. Those odors were part of the reason he hated riding in the two-form's vehicle. He sneezed three times in succession. The smell irritated his nose and lungs.

"Are you all right, sweet'ums?" Kirsten peered over the back of her seat.

"Maybe he's developing allergies," the two-form said.

"Only to you," Teller grumbled.

The two-form glanced at Teller, but from the two-form's expression, he'd understood exactly what Teller said this time.

What if the two-form was hampering Teller's ability to form a proper bond with Kirsten? Despite the two-form's assurance not to interfere with Teller, maybe he spoke falsely. The two-form had been a frequent visitor since before Kirsten and Kaley had rescued Teller and Penn from the four-foot prison. Maybe his canine side had already bonded with her, whether on purpose or inadvertently.

There were witches with full canine familiars. There were even witches who bonded with multiple familiars. Jo had bonded to the squirrels and mice who inhabited her home territory, which meant they were off limits for hunting. There were even witches who didn't have a familiar at all. However, Morticia never mentioned any tales of a witch familiar-bonding with any two-form.

If only there was a way to find out . . .

The vehicle rolled to a stop, and the queer heartbeat of the metal monster cut off in mid-thump.

"Maybe I should leave Teller in your car until we check out the house?" Kirsten said.

"I'm not leaving your cat out here," the two-form

said. "One, it's too cold for a house cat. Two, in case you hadn't noticed, I have an exhaust leak in this beast. His sneezing may be caused by the carbon monoxide. I'm not taking the chance of him accidentally suffocating by leaving my car running so he doesn't freeze to death."

Interesting. Was the two-form really concerned about his well-being? Or was this a ploy to ingratiate himself further into Kirsten's graces?

Kirsten peered over her shoulder at Teller. "See? He's a good guy."

Even if the two-form wasn't trying to curry her favor, he definitely succeeded. Teller chose to say nothing.

"Let's go see what Sheriff Birkheimer found," the two-form said. "At least, we can talk him into letting Teller and Penn inside the house."

Kirsten exited the vehicle and retrieved Teller from the back seat of the two-form's vehicle. The two-form had parked his vehicle behind a larger black vehicle with the yellow stars and stripes of the Holmes County Sheriff's Office in front of the Wilson den.

Kirsten approached the steps to the porch. Doctor Ethan's best friend Uncle Jimmy knelt in front of the door. He spread powder with a large brush on the lock and handle.

"Did you find anything, Sheriff?" the two-form asked.

Uncle Jimmy looked up at the two-form. "I've got a few prints. I'll compare them with the family's and yours." He shook his head. "I swear, Donald MacInnis Fryer, if you are trying to impress your girlfriend by leading us on a wild goose —"

The two-form held up his palms. "I swear on Mother Coyote I did not bring a tree over to the Wilsons' house. You can call the principal if you have to. I didn't skip school, and I've been at Jo's since the school librarian kicked me out this afternoon."

Uncle Jimmy snorted. "I've already checked the back door and the downstairs windows. If someone broke into the house, they were a professional."

"A professional?" The two-form knelt in front of the carrier and stared at Teller. "Is that what you were trying to tell me at the café? That Ellie and River broke into the house?"

"Yes," Teller hissed.

The two-form muttered a human curse word that would have gotten him hexed by Rachel if she had heard him.

"You guys got Rachel riled up because you didn't bother to ask the cats?" Uncle Jimmy said.

"It had to have been Ellie who picked the conventional locks," Kirsten mused. "Her aunt and uncle's powers would prevent any harm from coming to her, and River knows better than to use his fae abilities on Mom's protection spells."

Uncle Jimmy grunted. "Sounds like I need to have a word with St. James Coven's chief enforcer about one of his people breaking Normal laws."

The scents of Penn, Kaley, and Jo came from somewhere nearby. Teller couldn't see anything unless the door to his carrier faced in that direction. He was getting mighty tired of being in the stupid contraption. Not to mention it was far too cold to be outside while the humans blamed each other.

"For giving us a Yule tree?" Kaley said.

"Can't we please go inside and get warm?" Penn wailed.

"I second that motion!" Teller howled.

"The cats and I are freezing our furry butts," the two-form complained. "Are you finished dusting for prints?"

"You kids need to use the back door to go inside," Uncle Jimmy growled. "And you're making me some hot coffee for dragging me out here when your familiars were trying to tell you who was responsible the entire time."

Teller snuggled on Kirsten's lap on the couch and accepted the treats the two-form fed him while Uncle Jimmy paced in the kitchen as he spoke with Chief Enforcer Stanton. Kaley sat on one of the overstuffed armchairs and did the same for Penn. Jo sat on the other armchair and sipped her coffee.

"I'm sorry we didn't listen to you." Kirsten stroked Teller's fur.

He chewed and swallowed his treat before he said, "It would be easier if we had a real familiar-witch bond."

The two-form repeated to Kirsten what Teller said.

"But we are bonded," Kirsten protested.

"No," Jo said softly. "You're not."

"What do you mean?" Kirsten stared at her kinswoman. "I've had Teller for four years. I know what he's thinking—most of the time."

Teller laid his right front paw on her hand with the treats and shook his head like humans did.

"We don't?" His human looked crestfallen at his negation.

He shook his head a second time.

"Have you touched his mind?" Kaley said.

"You know how Dad feels about us using our telepathy on others," Kirsten replied.

"Honey, you've used your gifts in an emergency," Jo pointed out. "Besides, you and Kaley talk telepathically to each other all the time."

"That's different," Kirsten wailed. "Dad would kill us if he thought we forced ourselves into Teller or Penn's mind."

"You can't force the bond," Kaley said. "It has to be done jointly. With love. Even I know that." She shrugged. "According to Mom, sometimes, it takes a while."

The two-form muttered an obscenity. "No wonder he hates me. He thinks my coyote side has bonded with you instead of him."

"Yes," Teller admitted. The two-form repeated Teller's answer in human.

"Ewwww!" Kirsten stared at the two-form, then at Teller. "Sweet'ums, I would never do that to you."

Teller leapt onto the back of the couch and rubbed his cheek against Kirsten's non-furred one. "I love you."

She turned her head and looked him in the eyes. Suddenly, he could see his own visage from her point of view. Overwhelming warmth and love filled him to the tops of his ears.

Kirsten?

Wet droplets rolled from her eyes down her bare cheeks. *Teller? Oh, my gosh! I can hear you!*

"I can hear Teller," she shrieked.

Not so loud! Teller purred to calm her. *I'm right here.*

"What's the shouting about?" Uncle Jimmy barked as he walked into the living room.

"Kirsten and Teller have officially bonded," Jo said.

"I thought he was already her familiar." Uncle Jimmy removed his hat and scratched his head.

"There's a difference between a pet and a bonded familiar," Jo said dryly.

"Are you going to explain it to the poor Normal in the room?" Uncle Jimmy said.

"They have a permanent telepathic bond," Jo said. "Unless you're volunteering to be a familiar?"

Uncle Jimmy's face darkened. "I think I'll pass. I don't need impressionable young women in my head."

The front door slammed open. Teller jumped at the noise. But it was Rachel who stepped into the living room, her own face as dark as Uncle Jimmy's.

"I thought I told you girls to stay with Jo!"

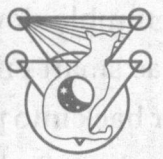

Chapter 4

Teller looked at Kirsten. *I've never seen your dam this angry before.*

Me neither. Kirsten continued staring at Rachel.

Jo looked around the back of the chair and said dryly, "The girls *are* with me."

Rachel spluttered in incoherent rage.

"Calm down, Rach, before you give yourself a stroke," Uncle Jimmy said.

Teller groaned at the same time as the two-form.

"Even I know not to say that to any woman, no matter her species," the two-form whispered to Teller.

"Then you've got a certain advantage," Teller said. "Because if you ever say that to my witch, I'd scratch your eyes out."

"Noted," the two-form whispered.

The scent of ozone filled the room, and Kirsten jumped to her feet, leaving Teller to tumble down to the couch cushions. The two-form was smart enough not to comment as Teller licked his fur back into place.

"Mom, if you even think about throwing a fireball at Jimmy, I will drench you in such cold water you'll have pneumonia for the rest of the winter." Kirsten's hands were raised, and Teller could hear every faucet in the house start running.

Kaley smirked at the showdown, and Penn snickered.

"If you'd give Jimmy and the girls a chance to explain, you'd know what happened," Jo said, her tone still dry as a desert.

Rachel took a deep breath, and her shoulders relaxed. "Someone broke into my home, and I want charges filed." She turned to the two-form. "I don't care what their intentions were."

"Why does everyone blame me when things go haywire?" the two-form growled.

"You're picking on the wrong boyfriend—" Uncle Jimmy started.

"We are not dating," Kaley protested.

"River and Ellie are behind the surprise tree delivery," Uncle Jimmy finished wryly.

The two-form's phone buzzed, and he jerked before he pulled the device from his pocket and held it to his ear.

"Hey, Mom!"

Teller could hear the two-form's dam. Her raised voice and rapid speech made it impossible to understand a word of what she was saying.

"Mom, the tree is a gift from River and Ellie. They left one at the Wilsons' place too before they flew out this afternoon."

His dam calmed down, but she protested the gift was too much for a couple of teenagers.

"Mom, Ellie's family is loaded, and I doubt her mom and stepdad would object to her spending a bit of her trust fund on two Christmas trees," the two-form said. "It's not like she left me a Maserati in our driveway."

The two-form's dam agreed. Upon hearing the two-form's words, Rachel looked abashed. The smell of ozone faded as both she and Kirsten canceled the spells they'd been about to launch.

"I'm at the Wilsons' now." A pause where Teller couldn't catch the words of the two-form's dam.

"I was at the café, but Mrs. Wilson was afraid their tree was some kind of trap set by Humanity Now, so I went with Jo and the sheriff to check it out."

Another pause. Teller had to give the two-form credit. He found the whole thing humorous, but he wasn't about to laugh in Rachel's face.

"Because none of us thought to ask Penn and Teller. They were here when River and Ellie brought the Wilsons' tree over. The sheriff called Ellie's step-grandfather to confirm everything was on the up-and-up."

A third pause.

"It's a long story. I'll explain it over breakfast in the morning. Love you." The two-form lowered the phone from his ear and tapped the glass with his thumb.

"Everyone, I apologize for . . ." It wasn't like Rachel to apologize, but then, she was so very rarely wrong.

"Overreacting?" Teller offered.

"Yeah, I got to agree with my familiar." Kirsten crossed her arms. "You went way over the top, Mom."

"Not to mention threatening a local law enforcement officer," Uncle Jimmy added.

"We know the Humanity Now frame-up scared you, Mom," Kaley said. "But you can't jump at everything little thing. Plus, you didn't give us any credit for checking the tree for spells. It was the second thing I did."

"Wh-what was the first?" Rachel choked out.

"I asked Kirsten if she knew anything about the tree."

46

"But not the cats." Jo chuckled.

Teller met Penn's gaze. "They're silly humans, but we still love them."

For once, Penn didn't have a smart reply. He rubbed his head against Kaley's arm and purred. The two-form repeated Teller's words for everyone who wasn't Kirsten.

"What did Ellie's grandfather say?" Rachel asked quietly.

"Chief Enforcer Stanton is meeting the jet when it lands in Las Vegas," Uncle Jimmy said. "River probably thought the whole episode was a romantic gesture for Kaley—"

"We're not dating," Kaley protested to no effect.

"—but Ellie knows better. I have a feeling she'll be grounded for the entire winter break."

"I'm still not sure I want this damn tree in the house after all the trouble it has caused," Rachel said.

"Why waste a perfectly good tree?" Jimmy tossed his hands in the air. "Is it because the tree probably came from the Slaughter's farm? It's not their fault that Simon's body was dumped on their property."

Rachel stared at the floor. It wasn't often she was wrong, Teller mused. But Uncle Jimmy had a point, and it obviously bothered her. She smelled like a mix of embarrassment and anger.

"Mom, River and Ellie tried to do something nice for us after all the crap we went through at Thanksgiving," Kirsten said softly. "Yeah, they probably went about it the wrong way, but their intentions were good. I get why you don't trust Normals right now. But River is one of us, and Ellie is Family."

Rachel faced Kirsten. "You have no idea what went through my mind last month when that mob came after you."

"Yes, she does Mom," Kaley said. "The same thing that went through ours and Dad's heads when you were arrested. The idea that we were about to lose you."

"I still don't want—"

Loud banging came from the back door. All the humans looked at each other with startled expressions.

"Ethan would have called you if he lost his house key, right?" Uncle Jimmy laid his hand on the butt of his gun.

"Oh Goddess." Kaley looked at Kirsten. "I left it unlocked when we came in the back door."

Teller jumped down from the couch and raced for the utility room. Penn jumped down from Kaley's lap and ran beside him. They reached the back door as it swung open.

A human male stepped inside. He dressed in red

leather coat and pants with matching boots and a cap. His white hair curled around his ears and blended into a full, fluffy beard. When he looked at the hissing cats, he smiled.

"Good evening, gentlemen. Your humans wouldn't happen to be here, would they?"

Teller turned to his brother. "Is it just me, or does he smell like a fae?"

Before Penn could answer, Uncle Jimmy charged into the tiny room, the gun in his hands aimed at the stranger.

"Put your hands up!"

Chapter 5

Teller whirled around, placing himself between Uncle Jimmy and the fae-smelling stranger. The stranger didn't just give off the honey scent signature of fae. Cinnamon, cloves, and evergreen mixed with the honey. With a start, he realized who the stranger was.

Kirsten, tell Uncle Jimmy to put his gun away, Teller said. *If he harms Father Winter, there will be a severe debt to the fae. He's human, but he's under their protection.*

"You have got to be kidding me," Kirsten replied. "Jimmy, holster your gun. You can't shoot Santa Claus!"

"What?" Uncle Jimmy's head swiveled back and forth between Father Winter and Kirsten.

"Thank you for vouching for me, Master Teller," Father Winter said. "Sheriff Birkheimer, Chief Enforcer

Stanton explained the situation with young Master River, and asked me to visit the Wilsons. Unfortunately, Master River hasn't learned all the rules regarding his father's heritage yet. Especially, those rules regarding gifts."

"Oh, my Goddess!" Kaley screeched. "Mom, do you have any idea what would have happened if you had thrown out the tree?"

"This is the reason I don't want you dating that boy!" Rachel shouted back.

"We are not dating!"

Penn rushed over to calm his witch.

A sharp clap of thunder knocked Teller over, but the humans stopped yelling at each other.

"Everyone needs to settle down." Jo's statement cut through the shocked silence. "Would you like a cup of coffee or tea while we calmly discuss the matter, Mr. Claus?"

Father Winter inclined his head. "I would be delighted to have some your exceptional coffee, Ms. Bice."

After fresh coffee was brewed for all the humans and Kirsten gave bowls of water and sugar cookies to the two reindeer hitched to a small sled in the back-yard, everyone gathered around the kitchen. Teller and Penn sat on their respective witches' laps to observe and comment on the proceedings.

"I literally just got off the phone with Alex Stanton." Uncle Jimmy had a bemused smile on his face. "How'd you get here so fast?"

Father Winter grinned. "That's a trade secret." He sobered abruptly. "Chief Enforcer Stanton called Master Gryffudd who called me."

This isn't good, Kaley said silently to Kirsten. *What do you think Master Gryffudd will do to River?*

Depends on if he follows Normal laws or fae laws. Kirsten oozed with worry. *I can't see a half-fae surviving long in a vampire coven if he followed Normal laws.*

Teller remained quiet, both mentally and verbally. It was rather entertaining being able to listen to both twins.

"Not even vampires and fae can dial a phone that fast." Uncle Jimmy laughed.

Father Winter made a point of turning and looking at the microwave. He turned back to face Uncle Jimmy.

"Technically, I won't get Master Gryffudd's call for another five minutes." Father Winter chuckled.

"You can time-travel?" Donny blurted.

"And my sleigh's bigger on the inside." Father Winter laughed heartily, though his flat belly didn't shake like in the human story. He quickly sobered. "The point is none of you have disposed of the tree, which is what Chief Enforcer Stanton was most concerned about."

"Because it's technically a fae gift, right?" Uncle Jimmy said.

Father Winter nodded.

"B-but fae gifts are cursed!" Rachel spat. "If we don't get it out of the house—"

Father Winter shook his head. "The rejection of the gift is a major breach of etiquette. If you insult a full-blooded fae by rejecting the gift, then yes, the gift automatically becomes cursed because they are easily offended. However, problems can occur in folks are part-fae and part-human. Especially in cases like River who hasn't been properly trained in his abilities. Teenage hormones don't help the matter. We are simply taking the appropriate precautions." He bit into a sugar cookie.

"But he broke into my house," Rachel protested.

"Be realistic, Rach," Uncle Jimmy said. "River's smart enough not to use fae magick on this house. He knows the damage fae and witch magick causes when they interact without safeguards. Ellie's the one who picked the lock. That's why I called Alex Stanton in the first place."

"River is an accessory then!"

Teller winced at Rachel's shouting. *Kirsten, I know your dam has a past with the fae, but why does she personally hate River so much?*

Good question. Kirsten repeated his inquiry to her dam.

"You've never had children, Teller," Rachel spat.

"Because you had your mate chop off my balls," Teller retorted. "You didn't answer my question."

The two-form was too busy laughing, so Kirsten had to translate. Both Uncle Jimmy and Father Christmas cringed at Teller's statement.

On the other hand, Rachel's mouth hung open.

"Teller's got a point, Mom," Kaley said. "Donny and Kirsten are actually dating, but you don't give him half as much crap as you give River. Who, by the way, made a relatively innocent mistake in trying to make our family happy after I tripped over a corpse on the Slaughter's farm. Which means your tirade obviously isn't just about him, so what's really going on?"

"When fae and weres cooperate to murder a goddess and witches help Normals kill other supernaturals—" Rachel let out a heavy sigh. "—I just don't know who to trust anymore."

"Not even me and Teller," Penn said in a soft voice.

Kaley repeated his words in human to her dam.

"When did you and Kaley bond?" Teller demanded.

"That's what I want to know," Kirsten added.

"This isn't about us," Kaley hissed before she turned back to her dam. "Mom, you're acting with the same insular view you complain about the rest of Millersburg having. If you don't ease up, you going to have more trouble than you know what to do with. I have no problem filing a racial harassment complaint with the International Council on River's behalf."

"Donny and I will back up Kaley," Kirsten proclaimed.

"The kids aren't the only ones who'd file a complaint with the IC," Uncle Jimmy added. "River lives under my jurisdiction. I won't put up with bigotry from you any more than I would from Humanity Now."

"Here's one more thing to think about," Jo added. "If Master Gryffudd is right and River is his half-brother, it means the kid's biological father was Duke Hoarancill of the Unseelie Court. If the kid's even half as powerful as his father, is River really someone you want to make an enemy?"

Blood drained from Rachel's face.

"Right now, River doesn't always consciously know

what he's doing," Penn said. "He emits the odor of cat-nip whenever he's here because he wishes to please me and therefore Kaley."

Kaley nearly choked on translating his words for her dam before she looked at her familiar with a frown. "Does he really do that?"

"Yes," Teller and the two-form said in unison.

"That's why it's good his learning to control his abilities from his fae family," Teller finished. "They appear to care about him and want him trained properly." Kirsten repeated his words in human.

"Consider also, Master St. James and his predecessor have taken in a contingent of halflings and exiled fae, all of whom are related in some fashion to each other and to River," Father Winter said. "They won't be happy about the way you've been treating the boy."

"All right, all right." Rachel held up her hands, palm outward, a human gesture of surrender. "I get the message. The tree will stay." She glared at each human and cat in turn. "However, I reserve the right to take it to the recycling plant when it dies."

Father Winter chuckled. "That may be longer than you wish, but I doubt River will object to that measure.

The back door knob rattled. The wood creaked, and a blast of cold pierced the cozy kitchen before the door closed again. Doctor Ethan entered the room, still wearing his heavy coat.

"I hate to ask this, but why are there reindeer in our backyard?"

door closed again. Doc as Ethan entered the room, still

would... ...ay coat...

...ith this, bursay ...ng the blunder in our

bac...

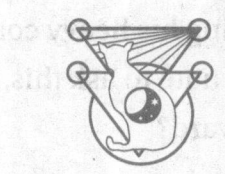

Chapter 6

Later that night, Teller followed his witch and the two-form into Penn and Kaley's room. They all gathered around Kaley's desk or on it while she spoke with animated hand gestures to the moving picture of River on her phone as she told him of her dam's overreaction to his gift.

River rolled his eyes. "I told Ellie sneaking into your houses was a bad idea, but she insisted we need to put them in water right away to keep them fresh."

"Rachel chilled out after the cats, the twins, the sheriff, Jo, Doc Wilson, and Santa Claus threatened to file complaints against her with IC on your behalf," the two-form said.

"Santa Claus?" River's eyes widened. "Are you kidding?"

"Nope," Kaley answered. "Apparently, when Uncle Jimmy called Chief Enforcer Stanton about Ellie, the chief enforcer asked Santa Claus to check on us."

River sighed. "I shouldn't be shocked after everything else that's happened this year. I don't know why I am surprised to learn Santa Claus really exists."

"You've had a lot to deal with," Kirsten murmured in a consoling tone.

"Speaking of a lot to deal with—" River audibly gulped. "I found out who my biological dad is. Or was."

"Duke Hoarancill," the girls and the two-form said at the same time.

"H-how'd you guys know?"

"Uncle Jimmy let it slip Chief Enforcer Gryffudd suspected you two are half-brothers," Kaley said. "I take it he had the results when you got there."

"I'm not sure how to handle the fact that my father was an assassin," River whispered.

"Dude, he was just doing the job his queen ordered," the two-form said.

"I doubt the Winter Queen commanded him to knock up my mom," River said sourly.

"At least he didn't betray his own people like my dad did," the two-form said equally sourly.

A bitter laugh echoed tinnily from the phone's

speakers. "Fine. You win in the crappy father department."

"Hey, you got a brother out of the deal," Kirsten said.

"Actually, two brothers and a bunch of cousins," River said wryly. "In addition to Stan, there's Jarunmisanrill. He's a full-blooded fae, but he got exiled when he and our dad failed to kill Ellie's aunt."

"And Ellie's aunt is okay with him being in the West Coast coven's territory?" Kaley said.

"Stan worked out a deal with her." River chuckled. "From what Stan told me, she'd probably side with your mom after what the fae tried to do her and her husband." He shrugged. "I could ignore my weird abilities most of the time, but meeting my brothers makes everything a little too real."

"Have you talked to your grandma about all this?" Kaley asked.

River nodded again. "She said she hoped I would come back to Millersburg, but she said she totally understands if I want to move to Las Vegas. Stan's wife Mai is pretty cool though. She said I could do whatever I wanted, and I shouldn't let Stan treat me like a child just because he's old enough to be my gazillionth great-grandpa."

All the humans laughed.

"I did ask Grandma if she would think about retiring and moving to Las Vegas when she was ready," River said.

"And?" Kaley's lower lip quivered. Teller could smell the anxiety and fear emanating from her.

"I'm coming back to finish high school at West Holmes," River said. "I'll visit my brothers on school breaks. I-I—"

"You what?" Kaley prodded gently.

"I don't want to abandon Mom, and I don't think Grandma does either." River's words exploded in rush. "After I graduate, I need to make some decisions, but until then, I'm taking this insanity one day at a time."

"One more thing before Kirsten and I leave you two alone to talk," the two-form said. "I don't usually comment on another guy's odor, but you have got to tone down the catnip smell you exude when you're here at the Wilsons. Penn is getting drunk off his ass from it."

"I am not," Penn yowled.

"Are too," Teller grumbled.

River gave an embarrassed laugh. "Yeah, I've already been told to work on my body chemistry." He shook his head. "I didn't realize how much I didn't know until Stan asked me what he called basic questions."

"But in his case, Normals still believed in the fair folk when he was your age," the two-form said. "He probably figured out what he was a lot sooner than you did."

"Among other things." River sighed again. "It's pretty late for me . . ."

"Good night, River," Teller said before he leapt down from Kaley's desk.

Kirsten and the two-form also said their farewells and followed Teller out of Penn and Kaley's room. No matter how much Kaley protested, even Kirsten knew her twin was in love with the halfling. Kirsten closed the bedroom door behind them.

"I'll be right back." She turned toward the upstairs bathroom.

Teller padded into their bedroom and jumped up on their bed. The two-form flopped down on his back beside Teller on the mattress.

"I told you I wasn't interfering with your familiar-witch bond," the two-form said.

"I'm not apologizing," Teller hissed. "You are interfering by spending more time with her."

The two-form rolled onto his side to face Teller. "I'm not spending any more time here than I did before we started dating. You know, like when you used to call me Donny instead of 'two-form.'"

Maybe the two-form, ur, Donny had a couple of good points.

"All right." Teller yawned and dropped on his side to stare at Donny. "I will use your given name from now on. But if you start mating with her on my bed, I will tell—"

"Rachel, and she'll curse me with fleas. I get it."

Teller snickered. "Nope. I'll tell Doctor Ethan, and I assure you he's very good at removing balls."

"You are a devil cat," Donny muttered.

"No." Teller cocked his head. "I'm a witch's familiar. I'm Kirsten's familiar. And I will protect here with my last breath."

"Then we're on the same side, my man." Donny laid his hand on the bed.

Teller placed his paw on top of Donny's palm. "I'm glad we agree on one thing."

"Happy Yule," Donny murmured.

"Merry Christmas," Teller replied.

And at the two-form's smile, Teller purred.

Divination
and
Distribution

The frigid January wind tried to find an egress in Donny Fryer's old brown hunting jacket while he threw a large tennis ball for Judge. The cold didn't seem to bother the huge German Shepard who raced after the furry neon green sphere. Donny suspected the dog could have leapt over the chain link fence surrounding the exercise yard behind the Millersburg Veterinary Clinic.

If he really wanted to.

However, Judge didn't seem to be inclined to leave the clinic. He got three squares, a warm place to sleep, and plenty of exercise. At least, he was no longer moping in his kennel like he had been after his human died from a massive heart attack the day after Christmas. Unfortunately, the poor dog currently existed in a legal limbo.

Saul Truman left his entire estate to Doctor Ethan Wilson, the senior partner at the clinic, on the condition the doc would care for Judge for the rest of his life. Except Teller and Penn, the cat familiars of Doc Wilson's daughters, weren't keen on the idea of a regular old Shepard in their house. Plus, Mr. Truman's kin crawled out of the woodwork when they learned how much money the old man really had. They had filed a challenge to Mr. Truman's will. None of his family gave a crap about Judge.

Judge raced back across the dormant grass and placed the slobbery ball next to Donny's boots before he looked up at Donny with a pleading expression.

Donny couldn't help laughing at Judge's antics. "Two more times, then we need to go inside. I've got to help Josh finish cleaning out the kennels."

"Two more's good," Judge barked. "Throw 'em hard!"

Donny grinned and threw the ball across the yard. Judge raced after it.

Donny shook his head. It was funny how well he understood other canines. But then, he was a werecoyote. Cat languages were a little harder to translate. But what startled him was overhearing a domestic squabble between the squirrels who lived in the tree outside his bedroom while he was doing his homework two nights ago. Apparently, female squirrels are just as uncomfortable during pregnancy as their human counterparts.

After Judge's last retrieval, he said, "I wish you didn't have to go. Why can't I go home with you? We would have a lot of fun."

"Sorry, dude." Donny scratched Judge behind his ears. "I'd love to, but I don't have the money to feed you."

"My human Saul said he'd make sure I had a home with Doctor Ethan, but he leaves me here every night."

"I know." Donny led the way to the back door of the clinic. "The doc is trying to get things sorted out, but humans have some weird rules."

Judge growled low in his throat, his opinion of the situation and the rest the Truman clan obvious.

They entered the kennel section of the clinic. From direction of the examination rooms came howling. A dog in such total panic they weren't making any sense

67

despite Doctor Wilson speaking in a low and soothing tone.

And Josh Fairbanks was nowhere to be seen.

"Someone's not happy," Judge said.

"Please get in your room." Donny opened the door to the German Shepard's kennel. "I need to get in there before someone gets hurt."

"Doctor Ethan wouldn't hurt one of us," Judge protested.

"I'm more worried about him getting his arm chewed off."

"Then I should go with you," Judge said.

"If you get hurt trying to help, I'll be in huge trouble."

Judge trotted into his kennel without another word. Donny latched the door and ran toward the ruckus. In Exam Room #2, he found Doctor Wilson trying to examine a white dog squirming on the stainless steel exam table while Josh and another schoolmate Hope Stillwell tried to hold the canine still.

The patient looked to by some kind of terrier mix, but bigger. While most of his fur was white, he had brown fur around his eyes and on his ears. But it was the dog's odor that gave away his true nature.

Donny locked the exam room's doors and shouted, "Let go of him."

"What are you talking about?" Doctor Wilson yelled over the canine's howling.

"Let him go! He's not a dog!"

That statement startled the three Normals and the were, who lay on the exam table and panted. Josh and Hope backed away from the exam table.

"Hope, would you mind turning your back for a moment?" Donny said. The were eyed him suspiciously.

"Rembrandt is just a stray I found wandering around our farm," she said. "I brought him in for the doc to check to see if he's been chipped because I put up signs all over town looking for an owner."

"And was he?" Donny raised an eyebrow.

"No, but—" Doctor Wilson sighed and rolled his eyes. "You have got to be kidding me. Josh, Hope, go to the waiting room." The veterinarian grabbed hold of the collar around the were's neck so he couldn't dash out the door.

Josh and Hope looked at each other before they nodded and left the exam room. Donny locked the door again.

"Here's the deal," Donny said. "I can smell what you are. You know what I am. You can trust the doc here because he's married to a supernatural. For that matter, you can trust both Josh and Hope. But if I find out you've been watching Hope naked while pretending to be a stray, you are in a world of hurt."

The white and brown dog whimpered.

"Not from me." Donny crossed his arms. "Hope is my girlfriend's best friend, and you don't want to be on the wrong side of my girlfriend. Now, change to human so the doc here can understand our conversation."

The dog leapt down from the exam table and retreated to a corner. Donny couldn't blame him. Mid-shift was the most vulnerable state for a were.

Flesh stretched. Bones cracked as ligaments and tendons rearranged themselves. The ears and snout shrank while the tail disappeared back into the were's body. The white and brown fur receded to show medium brown skin.

A boy, who couldn't have been more than twelve or thirteen rose to his bare feet. All he wore was the collar and a scowl. The scowl Donny recognized all too well. He'd seen the attitude enough times in bathroom mirrors.

The kid's chin jutted out. "If you call Child Services or ICE, I'll just run away again."

Acknowledgements

The past few years have been rather rough mentally and emotionally for our family. COVID-19. A lot of family deaths, including all of mine and Darling Husband's parents. A bout with breast cancer. Cataract surgery caused by the medication to prevent any cancer from spreading. Genius Kid's first overseas deployment. Plus, numerous things I will not mention. Go look them up in a history book.

If we still have those.

Through it all, I've had awesome friends who helped keep me sane. Thank you to Angie, Becky, Roshonda, Shelley, Jo, and Kim.

To my sprinting pals who tried to keep me honest, thank you to Candi, Tracie, Madi and Kate.

To Jaye and Elaina, who I owe for making my books look good, my deepest love and appreciation.

To my readers who still believe I write good stories, thank you for your support!

And most of all, much love to Darling Husband, Genius Kid, the Grandpuppy, and Princess Bella for their unconditional love and support.

Let us hope that peace, love, and kindness are not given in vain!

SUZAN HARDEN transitioned from writing infor-
mation technology manuals for companies and legal articles for a law enforcement magazine to her
first love, fantasy and science fiction in all their
forms. She's the author of the Millersburg Magick
Mysteries, the Soccer Moms of the Apocalypse series, and the Books of Apep series.

www.ingramcontent.com/pod-product-compliance
Lightning Source LLC
Chambersburg PA
CBHW010738100726
47899CB00009B/3099